DATE DUE

ABCDE
FG
K
M
O
P
Q
T
U
W X Y Z

To Erwin, Belové and Erill
– U complete my ABC.

Thanks Rain,
my little editor. –JJA

Thank you Rosalee
– it's been a pleasure.

Gertrude,
my niece, you inspire me! –EM

FriesenPress

Suite 300 - 990 Fort St
Victoria, BC, Canada, V8V 3K2
www.friesenpress.com

W $25.50

ISBN
978-1-4602-8022-5 (Hardcover)
978-1-4602-7656-3 (Paperback)
978-1-4602-7657-0 (eBook)

1. Juvenile Fiction, Concepts, Alphabet

Distributed to the trade by The Ingram Book Company

ABC,

ABC WHAT DO YOU SEE?

BY: JILL JAVELOSA-ALVAREZ, RECE

ILLUSTRATED BY: EL NIÑO MARTINEZ

ABC,
ABC what do you see?

We see **DEF** drinking some tea.

DEF, DEF
what do you see?

We see **GH|**
climbing a tree.

GHI, GHI what
do you see?

We see **JKL** chasing a bee.

JKL, JKL what do you see?

We see **MNO** going to ski.

MNO, MNO what do you see?

We see **PQR** dancing so free.

PQR, PQR what do you see?

We see **STU** playing at sea.

STU, STU what do you see?

We see **VW** counting to three.

VW, VW what do you see?

We see XYZ
finding a key.

XYZ, XYZ what do you see?

We see the LETTERS
singing with glee...

A B C D E F G H I J K L M N O P
Q R S T U V W X Y Z

Now, I know my **ABC** –
26 letters for you and me.

A B C D E
F G H I J K
L M N O P
Q R S T U
V W X Y Z

ABOUT THE AUTHOR

Jill Javelosa-Alvarez lives in Whitby, Ontario, with her husband Erwin and two children, Erill and Belové. She is a Registered Early Childhood Educator who currently works as an Early Literacy Specialist. A community advocate for children's literacy, Jill has run workshops that enhance children's literacy and numeracy development through play-based activities, she has recommended thousands of books to parents of children six years and under, and now she's written a book of her own that incorporates the early literacy skills she teaches every day.

In her leisure time, Jill and her family love traveling and exploring the outdoors. In 2015, Jill was a nominee for the Educator of Character award from the Character Community Foundation of York Region. Jill enjoys reading, photography and theatre arts.

CPSIA information can be obtained
at www.ICGtesting.com
Printed in the USA
LVOW05*1907020316

477520LV00016B/92/P